ANN JONAS

SPLASH!

GREENWILLOW BOOKS, NEW YORK

I have a pond in my backyard.
I have one turtle, two catfish,
three frogs, and four goldfish.
I feed them every day.

How many are in my pond?

My cat comes home.
He wakes my dog.
The turtle jumps into the pond.

SPLASH

How many are in my pond?

My cat watches the fish.
My dog chases the cat.
One frog jumps in. SPLASH

How many are in my pond?

My cat falls in.
My dog falls in. SPLASH
SPLASH

How many are in my pond?

My dog and cat climb out.
A dragonfly falls in. SPLASH
One frog hops out.

How many are in my pond?

Two frogs hop out.
My dog slips back in. SPLASH

How many are in my pond?

I help my dog out.
The dragonfly flies off.
One frog jumps in. SPLASH

How many are in my pond?

The third frog jumps in. SPLASH
The turtle stays in.
I climb out.

How many are in my pond?

My dog is sad.
My cat is mad.
I feed my fish.

The full-color illustrations were prepared in two parts. For the background, one painting was created and used for all scenes. For the action, a separate painting was done for each spread and mechanically combined with the background painting as part of the four-color separation process. Acrylic paints on clear acetate were used for all art. The text type is Akzidenz Grotesk.

First Edition 12

Library of Congress Cataloging-in-Publication Data
Jonas, Ann.
Splash! / by Ann Jonas.
    p.   cm.

"Greenwillow Books."

Summary: A little girl's turtle, frogs, dog, and cat jump in and out of a backyard pond, constantly changing the answer to the question "How many are in my pond?"

ISBN 0-688-11051-7 (trade)
ISBN 0-688-11052-5 (lib. bdg.)
ISBN 0-688-15284-8 (pbk.)
[1. Fishes—Fiction. 2. Animals—Fiction. 3. Counting.]   I. Title.
PZ7.J664Sp 1995 [E]—dc20
94-4110 · CIP   AC

For Don, Nina, Amy.
    Let me count the ways...